THE GREAT CHICKEN ESCAPE

NIKKI McCLURE

cameron kids

A NOTE FROM NIKKI

In June of 1998, I lived with a small group of monastics on Spruce Island, Alaska. When summer arrives in Alaska, there is work to do. Nuns dig the garden and nourish it with kelp lugged up from the beach. Salmon swim home in June. The nuns set a net and check it every six hours by kayak, pulling the caught fish onto their laps. Salmon are cleaned on the black rocks of the beach with shells. Fish guts are left on the beach for eagles, magpies, ravens, and foxes to eat. The salmon is canned or smoked for winter food. Later there is an island of kalina and salmonberries to pick and make a year's worth of jam, mushrooms to thread and hang in the heat of the kitchen fire, and peppermint to dry for a winter of tea. Then there are always the chickens to tend to: repairing the netting so magpies can't get in, collecting eggs, and listening to their gentle clucking.

Island life makes small events huge. I made this book to commemorate the day the chickens escaped. This is a true story, or as close to truth as I could ascertain from the chickens themselves. One day, the chickens sneaked out the back door of the coop. Some of the more timid were caught, but a rogue group successfully eluded the nuns. The nuns decided that there was no real danger, only the possibility of a great chicken adventure. They let the chickens roam, enjoying the freedom of the forest. There was no worry, for the chickens would return home to roost; after all, they are chickens.

I thank all the nuns and monks of Spruce Island for their immeasurable gifts.
I am full.

GOOD MORNING, CHICKENS.

CHICKENS RUN!

CHICKENS ROAM.

CHICKENS GO HOME.

CHICKENS, GOOD NIGHT.

FOR IAN

Copyright © 2018 by Nikki McClure
Book design by Melissa Nelson Greenberg

All rights reserved. No part of this book may be reproduced in any form without written permission from the publisher.

Library of Congress Cataloging-in-Publication Data available.

ISBN: 978-1-944903-22-0

The artwork for this book was created in 1998 by cutting black paper with an X-Acto knife.

This book is made with recycled paper.

Printed in China

10 9 8 7 6 5 4 3 2 1

Cameron Kids is an imprint of Cameron + Company

Cameron + Company
Petaluma, California
www.cameronbooks.com